WHITE HOUSE ADVENTURES

Secret
of the
Missing Teacup

Marianne Hering

Chariot Victor Publishing
A Division of Cook Communications

Chariot Victor Publishing
A division of Cook Communications, Colorado Springs, Colorado 80918
Cook Communications, Paris, Ontario
Kingsway Communications, Eastbourne, England

SECRET OF THE MISSING TEACUP
© 1998 by Marianne Hering

Edited by Kathy Davis
Designed by Andrea Boven
Cover illustration by Matthew Archambault

First printing, 1998
Printed in the United States of America
02 01 00 99 98   5 4 3 2 1

Library of Congress Cataloging-in-Publication Data

Hering, Marianne.
      Secret of the missing teacup/ Marianne Hering.
          p.   cm. – (White House adventures ; 1)
      Summary: Charlie Brooks, a black child, prays for God's help when
he goes to the new federal city of Washington to search for his father who
is working there, and ends up mixed up with President Adams, his granddaughter, and a proposed peace treaty with the French.
    ISBN 0-7814-3064-X
    1. Adams, John, 1735-1826–Juvenile fiction.   [1. Adams, John,
1735-1826–Fiction. 2. White House (Washington, D.C.)–Fiction. 3. Christian
life–Fiction. 4. Afro-Americans–Fiction.]
I Title. II. Series: Hering, Marianne. White House adventures; 1.
PZ7.H431258Se 1998
[Fic]–dc21
                                     98-8053
                                          CIP
                                          AC

To my father: Jack Ish Kendrick
Thank you for the countless hours you
spent lecturing me on minutia in Western
history. They weren't wasted.

CHAPTER

1

The Lost Coach

The coach door swung open. The little girl jumped out and ran as if she were a squirrel chased by a fox. The sash of her pink silk dress fluttered behind her as she dashed into the forest.

Next out of the coach was an older girl of ten. She was dressed as a housemaid, her long plain dress covered by a full white apron.

"Miss Adams," called the servant. "Come back here. The coach is just about to leave."

For an answer, the dark-haired Miss Adams ducked behind a bush and sat in the dirt. "I hate it in there," she cried. "We'll never get to Washington City."

The housemaid didn't try to reason with her. She took the girl by the arm and began to pull. At the first tug, the younger girl wrapped her free arm around an elm trunk and held on like a limpet to a rock.

The boy who was watching from behind the shelter of some oak trees couldn't help but laugh.

It was the servant girl who heard the noise and first

noticed him.

"Look!" the girl cried, pointing. "There's a black boy hiding behind the trees."

Suddenly little Miss Adams got up and ran back to the coach quick as a jackrabbit. The maid followed, watching the boy carefully. Her eyes held curiosity but no meanness.

The boy stepped out from behind two thick trees. He didn't want anyone to think he had been spying, though he had been watching the coach circle the Maryland woods for over an hour. The coachman and his helpers, called footmen, would put the coach on a path only to make a wrong turn and become stranded in the woods again.

A woman in fine clothes slowly lowered herself out of the coach and straightened her white lace shawl. Though she was old now, the boy could tell she had once been pretty. She smiled when she saw him.

Her gentle expression gave him courage to speak. "Ma'am, are you lost?" the boy asked.

"Aye, we are," she said. "We left Baltimore and lost our way in these woods two hours ago. I think you're a servant the heavens have sent to help us. Please, will you honor us by pointing the way to Washington City?"

"Yes, ma'am," he said. "My father works there. He makes bricks for the new federal buildings." The boy was proud of his father, even though he had not seen him in over six months.

"I trust that your father is a master brick maker," she said. "I am the first lady, Abigail Adams. The president and I are to reside in the President's Palace. Will you pleasure me by telling your name?"

"Charlie, I mean Charles Anthony Brooks," he answered, lifting his chin.

"Will you guide and direct our coach driver, Charles?" Mrs. Adams asked, smiling again.

"Yes, ma'am" Charlie answered. The first lady nodded and then stepped carefully into the coach, a footman helping by guiding her elbow. The housemaid followed the first lady. Just before the girl climbed in the coach, she turned and flashed a smile. Charlie thought it was for him, but he couldn't be sure. With her pale white hair and white cap, Charlie thought she looked like a summertime daisy.

Charlie told the coach driver how to find the postal route to Washington City. The man was glad to have directions. At first he smiled and nodded his head while the boy motioned with his hands and described the turns. The coachman's smile soon turned to a frown.

"I can't remember all those directions," he said. "There are too many turns, and I'll get lost again. You must take me to the road."

"I can show you," Charlie said, "but I can't take you to Washington City. I must be home before dark."

"That is fine with me," said the driver. "I want to be well on my way before dark too."

So the young black boy pulled himself up in the seat next to the coach driver. From inside the coach came the servant girl's voice, "A boy has all the good fortune. God punishes girls by making us always stay safe and calm.

Why am I never allowed to ride outside?"

"Or me?" asked four-year-old Miss Adams.

Charlie couldn't hear any more words coming from inside the coach when the horse hooves began to thud on the damp ground. The large coach with four horses moved slowly through the thick woods of elm, white oak, and maple. Charlie felt important leading the way on the hard-to-follow road. It was just two brown patches of dirt where a few wagon wheels had cut a path. He sat up straight. *What an honor,* he thought, *to be helping the first lady. God surely must watch over her and listen to her prayers.*

When they reached the road, the coachman paid Charlie a handful of coins. Then Charlie jumped down from the seat and waved good-bye to the driver. The little girl opened the coach door and pushed her head outside. "Bye-bye," she said and waved back. In her hand was a toy-sized teacup, cream-colored with a wide gold rim. Then she and the teacup disappeared into the coach, and the door closed.

The boy thought that would be the last time he would ever see the president's family and servants again. He suddenly felt sad as he headed for the shack where he lived with his mother and his three sisters. He thought about how fun it would be to live in a growing city like Washington. Nothing exciting ever happened on the small tobacco farm he worked on.

If he lived in Washington City, he might find someone to teach him a trade. In Washington City, he would get to be with his father again.

Charlie was right in the middle of a daydream about

working side by side with his father when he saw something unusual lying on the dirt path. He bent down and gently picked it up. It was a white china teacup with small red flowers, just the size for tiny fingers. It had landed in a mud puddle, and Charlie saw that it had a crack and a tiny chip on the handle. *Miss Adams must have dropped this*, he thought. *I wonder if she will miss it?*

Then Charlie got an idea. *What if I take this to the President's Palace? Then I can see Father again!*

The rest of the trip home, Charlie's daydreams turned into firm plans to visit the federal city as soon as he could. He barely noticed the two men who passed him on the path riding on beautiful red horses.

They spoke in French and Charlie could only understand a few words. One of them said *President Adams*, and both men laughed. Charlie had the feeling the Frenchmen didn't like the president. He shivered as they rode away. He was glad they were going in the opposite direction. He hoped he would never meet them again.

CHAPTER

2

Danger on the Bridge

Charlie's dream to visit Washington City came true. Four days later, he rode in the back of a farmer's wagon. It was more than thirty miles to Washington City from the Brooks' shack in Maryland. The farmer was going as far as Georgetown. Charlie had to ride in the wagon with some chickens, but he didn't mind. He was thankful for the ride and hummed part of a hymn he'd learned at church.

He thought of how happy little Miss Adams would be when she got her teacup back. And he thought of seeing his father again.

"Go ahead and go," his mother had said when Charlie had told her his plans. "It will be one less stomach to fill while you're gone." But on the day he left, she hugged him tightly, and there were tears in her eyes when she said good-bye. Charlie knew that his mother wanted to go too, but she had to stay on the farm where she worked as a cook. His mother had made him wear his best clothes: a pair of brown breeches, an off-white shirt, wool stockings, and plain, sturdy leather shoes that came up to his ankles.

After he got out of the wagon in Georgetown and said good-bye to the farmer, Charlie had only two miles to walk before reaching Washington City. The closer he got to the federal city and the Potomac River, the more and more wet marshland he had to cross. In some places the road was covered so deep in water that his shoes and stockings got soaking wet. The damp smell of rotting plants and murky water soured the air.

He sat down on a plank bridge, just outside of the federal city. He put down the small drawstring pouch he had been carrying. In it were some food, the teacup, a razor, and some soap his mother wanted him to give his father. He had twenty-five cents of his own, part of what the coach driver had given him. His mother had kept the rest of the money.

Charlie slipped off his muddy shoes and stockings. He was going to see if he could dump the water out and squeeze the wetness out of his stockings. If that didn't help, he was going to walk barefoot.

Shoes were so expensive that Charlie was lucky to have a pair at all. His father had bought them two sizes too big so that Charlie wouldn't grow out of them so quickly.

He stuffed his wet stockings into his pouch. He was just about to stand up when he heard a voice from behind him. "Who's sitting on Willard's bridge?"

Charlie turned and saw two of the toughest teens he had ever met. One of the boys had upper arms as big around as a roast ham. The other was missing most of his front teeth. Toothless had scrunched up his face tight as a dried apple. He said, "What are you doing on Willard's bridge?"

"What does it look like?" asked Charlie. "I'm just taking off my shoes. Is there a law against it?"

"There sure is," said the teen. "I'm Willard, and this here is my bridge. You have to pay me if you want to cross it. That's *my* law."

Charlie was beginning to get worried. He didn't think he could fight off even one of the youths. He certainly could not fight both at once. Besides, his mother and father had taught him to fight with words, not fists.

Charlie searched for words now. "Did you build this bridge?" he asked Willard.

Both of the teens began to laugh. They were not friendly laughs, and Charlie stood up in his bare feet. He held his pouch underneath one arm. He left the muddy shoes lying on the bridge.

"It's none of your business if we built it or not," said Willard. "We own it now. You can either pay twenty cents or get off. If you want to be able to pass it anytime, you can pay two dollars."

The teen with the big arms stood at one end of the bridge. Willard stood at the other, blocking his way to the federal city. Charlie was trapped. He didn't want to give up twenty cents. It would take him a whole day's work just to earn it back—if he could find work. Two dollars was impossible. He had never had a whole dollar at one time in his entire life.

"I won't pay a bribe," Charlie said. "Next time you'll just want more."

"So he has got money," Willard said and nodded to his friend. "Sam, get his pouch."

Just as the strong youth took a step toward him, horse hooves pounded on the wooden planks of the bridge.

"Get out of our way," a man said with a French accent. The horse came so close to Sam that he jumped off the bridge in order not to get trampled. Charlie scooted to the edge of the bridge, but did not jump into the water. Willard moved aside just in time. Another man and a horse followed the first one. Both horses were deep red, and both men were dressed in black capes and black hats.

Charlie saw his chance. By keeping the horse between him and Willard, Charlie used the horse as a shield. He was a little afraid of getting trampled, but he was more afraid of Willard. Charlie ran alongside the second horse and got off the bridge. With his pouch in one hand, he sprinted as fast as he could away from the rough youths.

When Charlie finally looked back at the bridge, both were still near it. Willard was holding one of Charlie's shoes and shaking it in anger.

I may have lost my shoes, Charlie thought, *but at least I have the teacup.*

CHAPTER
3

Men in Black

After running far away from the bridge and the two angry teens, Charlie spotted the President's Palace. It stuck out like a white lily in a bed of weeds. The house stood alone on the countryside with a few small farmhouses tucked here and there around it. Scrub oak trees and orchards speckled the rest of the nearby area.

Since Charlie was only a boy, and a poor black one at that, he knew he should not go to the front door of the President's Palace and knock. Even if he had wanted to, it was almost impossible. In front of the large stone house was a deep pit covered only with a few thin planks. Some workmen were fixing up the entrance. One of them told Charlie to go around the side to the basement door.

Charlie walked carefully across boards that had been laid across large mud puddles. The smell of decay and rotting food surrounded him. He circled around piles of rubble and garbage, chasing away some muddy hogs that were eating anything they could chew. When he got to the door, he rapped three times.

14

"It's about time," a woman's sharp voice called out. The door opened, and Charlie saw an old servant wearing a white apron over a dark blue dress. The apron sash had quite a long way to circle her round body. She wasn't smiling, and a frown grew on her face as she studied him.

"Where are my black birds?" she asked.

Charlie just stood, looking inside. The stones and wood had been painted white. The place smelled of burnt oil mingled with wet clay and charred oak. The orange floor was made from brick like the kind used for fancy roads or walkways of rich people's churches. He wondered if his father had made any of those bricks.

He also wondered at the size of the room. Six shacks like the kind his family lived in could easily have fit inside. It was like a barn. All that space for one kitchen!

The woman shook his shoulder. "Well, are you going to tell me where the birds are or not?" she demanded in a tone that meant hurry up.

"I don't know anything about black birds, ma'am," Charlie said looking into her gray eyes. "I've come to speak to the first lady on . . . on . . . family business." He hugged his small pouch close to his chest.

"Family business!" she laughed. She wanted to poke fun at him. "As if you could be any part of a fine family like the Adamses. Family indeed! Your skin is the color of a potato before it's been washed. Family!" The housekeeper wanted to say more, but she couldn't stop laughing.

Just then the housemaid from the coach stepped out from behind the large oven. Her apron was stained and limp as if she had been wearing it for days without a washing.

"Listen to him, Aunt Esther," she said. "This boy helped Her Excellency—he helped us all get out of the woods."

The woman's body continued to shake with laughter, but she let Charlie step inside. She closed the door behind them and said, "Now suppose you tell me what you've got to do with the president's family before I throw you out with the pigs."

Charlie was disappointed that he was not going to get to see the first lady again. He knew that once this pushy woman had the teacup, he would have nothing to talk to Abigail Adams about.

Charlie began his story. "My name is Charles Anthony Brooks. And I told the coach driver . . ."

The old housekeeper interrupted him, narrowing her eyes. "I heard about that," she said. "Are you looking to be paid again?"

"No!" he said. "I've come to bring back the little girl's teacup. She must have dropped it."

"Bless you!" the woman cried. "Miss Adams has been crying about it for days. This is an answer to our prayers!" She took a step toward Charlie. "Where is it? Show me."

Charlie opened his pouch and removed the wet stockings. Then the woman peered inside. He saw the top of her white cap that was tied under her chin. It was like a dandelion fluffed into its white crown. She saw his lump of cornbread, several walnuts, and three apples. The teacup was wrapped in his mother's Sunday handkerchief and sitting next to the soap and razor. He slowly unfolded the cloth.

"Here it is, ma'am" he said, holding out the treasure. Against his rough blistered palm, the cup looked dainty and fragile.

"You can call me Mrs. Briesler," she said, smiling. Her teeth were straight, but grayed by tea stains. She turned toward the younger servant girl. "Hannah, take this to Miss Adams right away."

Before she left, the girl gave Charlie another smile. This time Charlie was sure it was for him and that it meant friendship. Then the girl vanished up a staircase.

Mrs. Briesler said, "That teacup is the first good news we've had since the first lady arrived. You deserve a reward."

His reward was food. Charlie left the kitchen with a stomach full of potato and cheese soup. His pouch was heavier, too. Mrs. Briesler had given him some biscuits, dried meat, and a bit of cheese to carry with him.

She had also given him hope of finding his father quickly. She sent him on his way after giving him directions to where the brick makers' shacks were.

Dare I hope that God will guide me and that I will find my father quickly? Charlie wondered.

He did find the shacks easily. There were twenty or so that shared walls and a thin roof. They were lined in a row near a creek. He found many black slaves hauling sand out of the water to make bricks. He asked several men if they knew a Curly Brooks. Some shook their heads. Most said, "There aren't any freemen working on bricks, only slaves."

Two asked, "Don't you mean old Walter Brooks?" But from their description, Charlie knew that it was not his father.

A sudden evening chill took Charlie by surprise. In November, night came early and cold, and he needed a place to sleep. He hadn't even brought a blanket with him because he had been so sure that he could share a bed with his father.

He knew a place in Georgetown where he could stay with friends. But he would first have to cross Willard's bridge. He didn't want to get his money stolen. Or get himself beaten up. Or killed.

He found himself walking up and down on the path to the President's Palace. He didn't have enough courage to knock on the kitchen door and ask for shelter. The girl would let him in, he was sure of it. But what if Mrs. Briesler opened it—or worse, a stranger? Mrs. Briesler had been fair to him, but she was a busy woman. He didn't want to bother her without a good reason.

And he didn't want to bother God. *Why would God care about a poor boy like me?* Charlie wondered. *God cares about the teacup of an important young girl, but He certainly didn't help me find my father today.*

Suddenly, as if swooping down from the sky, two horses with riders dressed in black surrounded him on the path. The horses were excited, and they stomped their hooves. Their breath flowed hot and turned to steam. For a moment, Charlie thought they were dragons.

"Are you going to the President's Palace?" a man

asked him in a heavy French accent.

"Pardon me, sir," said Charlie, confused by the man's hard-to-understand words. Charlie thought they were the Frenchmen who had ridden across Willard's Bridge and passed him on the road from Georgetown. He couldn't be sure because their faces were covered by the high collars of their capes and by their dark hats.

"Here," said the man very slowly in perfect English, "take this letter to His Excellency." He laughed. "Your honorable president."

Charlie shivered when he heard the mean laughter as the two men rode away on their horses. The boy was sure he had heard those voices when the men had passed him on the road some four days ago.

Charlie looked at the letter in his hand. He held another reason to go to the Adams' new home.

This time, Charlie thought, *I have a feeling that I won't be bringing good news.*

CHAPTER

4

The Mysterious Letter

Charlie stood in front of the President's Palace and wondered what to do about the mysterious Frenchmen and the letter. He wasn't tempted to open the envelope. He couldn't read English very well, and he didn't know a word of French. He didn't so much as peek.

After tucking the paper into his pouch, he hurried around to the back door. In his haste, he slipped on a plank, and one foot dropped into a deep, muddy hole. His breeches were sopping by the time he knocked on the door.

A man with a long nose opened it. His face reminded Charlie of a hound. The man wore a dark suit with a short jacket. "May I help you?" the steward asked.

"I brought a letter for the president," Charlie said. "I think he needs to read it right away."

Mrs. Briesler's voice could be heard from somewhere in the large kitchen. "If it's the man with my blackbirds, don't pay. I already made catfish." She came around to the door in a hurry. "Oh, it's Charles."

The man turned to Mrs. Briesler. "May I let him in?"

"Of course," she said.

Charlie stepped in on the red brick. All three of them looked down at the puddle made by his dripping breeches.

"This will not do," Mrs. Briesler said. "Come in next to the fire to dry off."

A weak flame was burning in the large fireplace. Charlie moved near it. He got as close as he could, but the small fire didn't warm him.

"Sorry we can't make the fire larger," the housekeeper said, "but we don't have much wood left. It takes thirteen fires to keep the President's Palace dry and warm. It's more important to keep the upstairs fires hot for His Excellency."

Charlie fanned the sides of his breeches to dry them more quickly. As he was flapping, Hannah came down the stairs and entered the kitchen. "Miss Adams wants more crackers . . ." She stopped talking when she saw Charlie, a wondering look in her eyes.

Mr. Briesler answered her silent question. "This lad is here with important business. Now where is this letter?"

Charlie told the Brieslers and Hannah about the two Frenchmen on horseback.

"*You* were chosen as a secret messenger!" Hannah muttered. "I pray to God every night for some excitement, and what do I get? To scrub the floors."

Charlie thought he could live very well without such excitement as he pulled the letter from his pouch. It was in an envelope sealed with pale wax. The housekeeper gently took it from him.

"This is fine paper," said Mrs. Briesler. "It could be important."

Mr. Briesler snatched the letter from his wife. Then he smoothed his jacket and straightened his white wig. "I'll give this to His Excellency right now."

Mr. Briesler hurried up the narrow staircase. Turning once, he was out of sight. Charlie feared Mrs. Briesler would ask him to leave at any moment.

As if reading his mind, Hannah asked, "Do you need a place to sleep tonight?" Her voice was soft.

Charlie nodded, but he looked at the brick floor.

"Did you find your father?" Mrs. Briesler asked.

Charlie shook his head.

"Well, you can't stay here," Mrs. Briesler said. "The servants' quarters aren't done. There's nothing but rubble in them, and the walls have not been plastered. My husband and I sleep down here in the basement. Hannah keeps watch over Miss Adams upstairs."

"There's always the stables," Hannah suggested.

Mrs. Briesler nodded. "Aye, there's the stables."

Just then Mr. Briesler's voice came down the twisty staircase. "Bring His Excellency something to drink in the drawing room," he yelled. "The president has had a shock. More firewood. Hurry."

In a flash, the housekeeper dropped a load of dry oak logs into Charlie's arms. "Come with me," she said. She grabbed a fancy crystal bottle and hurried up the stairs.

"I'm not staying behind and missing the fun," said Hannah. "I'm coming too."

The staircase was so narrow that Charlie banged the walls two or three times with the logs. After climbing dozens of steps, he followed the folds of Mrs. Briesler's dark skirt into a huge oval-shaped room. The fancy furniture and window coverings were a rich red color. Two dozen chairs and some sofas made from fine dark wood were placed against the walls. Though the room wasn't finished, Charlie could see that it was going to be grand.

The president was not as tall as Charlie imagined he would be. He was as round as Mrs. Briesler and bald on top for the most part. He wore his powdered hair pulled back in a ponytail. The lines on his face made him look every day the grandfather he was.

Charlie bent to place the logs on the fire, and Hannah sank down on her knees beside him. She had brought a pail and shovel to scoop out ashes. As they worked side by side, they heard soft footsteps on the wooden floor. It was the first lady. She wore a deep blue dress that had lace at the end of the long sleeves.

"My dear Mr. President," she said, "I came as soon as I received Mr. Briesler's call. You look ill. Tell me, is there grave news?"

"It is serious indeed," the president said. "I want your advice on this matter. He began to read the letter:

"Dear Mr. President:

We are the men who burned down the War Department building earlier this month. Unless you want to see your Capitol building destroyed too, you will listen to us. Send us 10,000 dollars in silver.

"If you are willing to give us the money, hang something white from the east window in the morning. If we do not see something white, we will plan a new danger."

John Adams continued, "It is signed 'Mr. X and Mr. Z.'"

"Can it be the same men from the XYZ affair?" Mrs. Adams wondered aloud.

Charlie turned to Hannah. Her eyes looked as wide and round as the full moon. Charlie knew his eyes must be filled with fear too. *What is the XYZ affair?* he wondered.

"I'm afraid it *is* those evil men," the president said. "And at least two of them have come here. It wasn't long ago they tried to get bribe money from the United States. Mr. X, Mr. Y, and Mr. Z said the United States had to pay them or France would destroy our ships. Maybe they think that I will give them the money if they threaten to destroy our new Washington City. They are trying to start a new XYZ trick!"

"But the peace treaty with France will be signed any day," cried Abigail Adams. Her hands were clasped near her throat. "You did everything you could to keep the French happy without giving up the country's honor."

"The United States won't pay a bribe," the president said, as he slammed his fist onto the arm of his chair. "I don't want war, but to pay them money would be against the freedom our country stands for. I have already built up our Navy in case they attack us at sea."

The first lady asked, "Are they serious about the evil deeds they speak of?"

"It seems they take credit for burning the War Department building," the president said, rubbing his chin. "What is to stop them from destroying something else? People who ask for bribes only want more money later. Even if I pay, we may indeed be heading for war."

CHAPTER

5

The Spy

Charlie's head was full of the XYZ mystery as he walked to the stables where Mrs. Briesler said he could spend the night. The stables were two full blocks away from the President's Palace. Charlie walked there alone in the dark. There were no roads, walkways, or lights from nearby buildings to guide the way. Every once in a while, he stepped on a sharp rock, and he wished for his shoes. He knew wild animals roamed nearby, and he didn't want to meet a bear. He pulled a wool cape tightly around himself.

"We'd give you a real blanket, but Her Excellency's things haven't yet come from Philadelphia," Hannah had explained earlier. "The president's household goods are on a ship. This cape is the only extra thing we have that will do for warmth. Be thankful Aunt Esther—that's Mrs. Briesler to you—parted with it. 'Tis not like her to be so kind to strangers."

Charlie nodded to her, and gave her a smile. He hoped it was as bright as the one she gave him. Then he left for the stables.

After arriving, Charlie realized that he wasn't the only one to sleep near the horses. Even if they smelled of horses, the stables were warm. Three other men were already there, though Charlie couldn't see their faces in the darkness. They were curled up and covered by blankets like squirrels wrapped up in their tails.

Charlie accidentally stepped on one man's ankle. The man sat up and called, "Who's there?"

Charlie recognized the coachman's voice and reminded him of their meeting in the Baltimore woods.

"You are far from home, lad," he said. "What brings you to the federal city?"

"I am looking for my father," Charlie said. He didn't want to tell anyone else about the teacup or the letter. "Mrs. Briesler said I could sleep here because I helped the first lady find her way out of the woods."

"What's your father's name?" a man at the back of the stables asked. Charlie tried to see his face, but he could not because of the shadows.

"Curly Brooks," Charlie answered.

"Never heard of him," the man said.

All three men ignored him after that. There was hardly any space in the stable with the men, twelve horses, two carriages, Mrs. Adams' coach, and all the food and equipment for the horses. Because it was too dark for Charlie to find an out-of-the-way spot, he plopped down on a stretch of clean straw near the door. He shaped a mattress out of the straw and tucked his pouch into one pocket of the old cape.

That night Charlie prayed before he fell asleep. He

asked God to help save the country from war with France. At the end, he asked God to help him find his father, and for a new pair of shoes. But he didn't really think God would pay attention to a poor boy like him when He had all the problems of the new country to take care of.

Then Charlie fell asleep, but he didn't sleep well. All through the night he dreamed that Mr. X and Mr. Z were chasing him on large red dragons with fire breathing out of their nostrils.

In the morning, the noise the other men made startled him out of sleep. He sat up, blinking. Straw was sticking out of his dark, springy hair. There were only two men in the stables. One must have stepped over Charlie and left during the night.

The coachman said to Charlie, "We've got to take His Excellency to view the federal property today. He wants to check the work on the Capitol building. Our president has to travel in style. That's the way he likes it."

Charlie moved from the door to allow the men to go outside. The coach driver said, "See that carriage and the silver harnesses, lad?"

"Yes," Charlie said.

"The carriage used to have a beautiful coat of arms painted on the side," the man said. "His Excellency loved it. It made him feel like royalty. That's the way they do it for the king in England. But of course, His Excellency had to paint over the coat of arms. The people of the United States don't want a king or anything to do with royalty. They want a plain old president."

Charlie bent down to pick up Mr. Briesler's cape and

his pouch. He checked to make sure everything was still in it, and he hurried off to the President's Palace to see if there was work to be done.

When he got there, Charlie found out that he wasn't the only one who had dreamed in the night. Hannah had formulated a plan for Charlie. And she was waiting outside the basement door to tell it to him.

She began talking before he could even say good morning. "The way I see it is that you need to find your father, and we need a servant to get some more wood."

Charlie nodded.

"Why don't you help us by finding wood and tending the fires? I don't have the time because I have to watch Miss Adams. I'm even behind on doing the laundry."

Charlie noticed her apron was even dirtier than the day before. He didn't feel so bad about not having shoes.

"Mrs. Briesler would have to ask me," Charlie said.

"I could fix it," she said. "Mrs. Briesler is my aunt. We already have a lot of work and no help."

"Well," Charlie said, "if she were to ask me, I'd be glad to tend the fires in the President's Palace."

The two went inside together. Mrs. Briesler offered him breakfast. Charlie sat at a small table and ate the leftover pieces of the president's catfish dinner. He saw Hannah motion to her aunt. Then the girl tiptoed and whispered in the old woman's ear. Charlie was not surprised when Mrs. Briesler walked over to him, hands on hips.

"It has come to my attention," she said, "that we need some firewood."

His mouth was too full for him to speak, so Mrs. Briesler kept on talking. "We'd hire you by the day, you understand. And while you're gathering, I wouldn't mind if you took a look around for your father. Has he written your family, telling where he is?"

"No," said Charlie after swallowing, "but that doesn't make any difference. My father can't write."

"Has he sent any money then?" she asked.

"No, ma'am. We don't have anyone we'd trust to do that."

"Well," Mrs. Briesler sighed, "I suppose your Heavenly Father will watch over you while you're looking for your earthly one."

Charlie wished he could believe that God cared about him enough to help him find his father. *God will forget about me,* he thought.

Just then the first lady came into the kitchen. Her bonnet was covered in ribbons and lace, and her dress was a beautiful green with a large flower pattern stitched around the hem. "Esther," she said to Mrs. Briesler, "I have it on good counsel that visitors will come today. It would please me to use the ivory and gold china."

"I can't find it," Mrs. Briesler answered. "I've emptied all the boxes that came in your coach and the wagons that followed it, and it's not there."

"But I packed it myself," the first lady said. "It's in a sturdy crate marked 'ivory china.' Please look again. It could be anywhere in this mansion. It is the biggest house in the country!"

The first lady started to go up the stairs, but stopped

and turned to Hannah. "The laundry needs to be done today as well."

Hannah nodded and curtsied to show that she was willing to do the first lady's bidding.

Charlie felt a little shiver when the first lady left, and he looked at the fire. The large kitchen was heated by a small heap of coals that had almost burned to ash.

"I'll bring the firewood," said Charlie. "You'll be warm tonight." He smiled at Mrs. Briesler and Hannah.

"I hope so," said Mrs. Briesler.

As he left the kitchen and headed out to the muddy paths of the federal city, Charlie watched his every step to carefully avoid stepping into any holes. And from behind a nearby farmhouse, someone else was watching Charlie's every step just as carefully.

CHAPTER

6

The Mistake

It only took Charlie an hour to collect his first load of firewood. He did his job as fast as he could to please Mrs. Briesler, who was letting him work as a servant at the President's Palace. As he carried his first load of firewood to the President's Palace, something in a window caught Charlie's attention. Laundry was hanging in one of the large rooms. It could be seen from far away. *Is that a signal for Mr. X and Mr. Z?* Charlie wondered. *The message said to hang something white in the window if the president was going to pay the bribe. Those linens are white as cotton!*

When he got to the kitchen, Mrs. Briesler was busy boiling some herbs. Hannah was nowhere to be seen.

"The first lady and little Miss Adams are both ill," she said. "You'll have to run over to Georgetown for us. There is no place to buy medicine in this new city. Mrs. Adams' joints ache, and the girl has a cough. Hannah has her hands full keeping the girl inside."

"I'll go," Charlie said.

"Can I trust you with money?" Mrs. Briesler asked.

"Yes, ma'am," he said.

"Aye, I can," She nodded. "I must give you a chance. This house needs thirty servants, not just Hannah, my husband, and me. There's so much to be done, I *have* to trust you. Hannah can't go as she's a girl. I would send the footmen, but they are out with the president in his carriage."

She put the money in his hand and told him what kind of medicine to buy in Georgetown. "Use the cape," she said. "It may snow."

Before Charlie left, he went to find Hannah. Hannah was just coming down the stairs as he was going up.

"Why did you hang the laundry in that room?" he asked. "You know it could signal Mr. X and Mr. Z. The president and first lady will be furious."

"I didn't think!" she said. "That's where we always hang it." Her hand flew up to cover her small pink mouth.

Charlie saw her pale blue eyes fill with tears. Then she turned and fled up the stairs.

When Charlie left the President's Palace, he saw Hannah through the window yanking down the clothes. No matter that they landed on the dusty floor. They had to be got down as soon as possible.

As he turned toward the road to Georgetown, the worry about the white clothes had made him forget about Willard's Bridge. But he didn't forget for long. When Charlie saw the youths again, the first thing he noticed was that Willard was wearing his shoes. Charlie slowed his walk as he came nearer the bridge.

"What's the matter?" Willard asked, showing his gap-tooth smile. "What are you so afraid of? All you have to do is pay forty cents, and we'll let you cross."

"It was only twenty cents yesterday," Charlie argued.

"But you didn't pay, did you?" Sam said. "We want yesterday's money, too." He slapped his right fist into his left palm. The message was clear: Pay or we'll beat you up and take your money.

Charlie quickly added up the money he had with him. With his own twenty-five cents and the money Mrs. Briesler had given him, Charlie had almost a dollar. If he paid the forty cents, he might not have enough to buy the medicine. He would have to go back without it, and Mrs. Briesler would think he stole some of the money.

Then he made a plan. The coins Mrs. Briesler had given him were not in his pouch. The medicine money was in the cape's pocket. If he threw the pouch into the wide Rock Creek, Willard and Sam might think it had coins in it. They would go after the pouch and leave him alone. Then he could cross the bridge, and he would still have enough money to buy the medicine. Charlie didn't like the thought of losing his pouch and his own twenty-five cents, but it was the only plan he had.

Charlie hurled the pouch with a quick snap of his arm. The pouch sailed through the air. It hit the water with a splash.

Both Willard and Sam watched it sink into Rock Creek. Sam laughed and said, "You don't think we're going to fall for that old trick, do you?"

Charlie prayed silently as he backed off the plank

bridge on the Washington City side. *God, please help me. Send your angels to protect me. I am on a job for the first lady and her granddaughter. Surely you care about their business even if you don't care about mine.*

Willard said to Sam, "He's got the money on him. Probably in that black cape. You get one arm, and I'll get his other. Don't let him get away!"

Charlie stepped off the bridge and turned to run. But the cape was too long for him, and it wrapped around his legs. He fell facedown in the dirt. He closed his eyes and held his breath. He waited for Willard and Sam to jump on his back, but nothing happened.

He opened his eyes when he heard some grunting and the sound of a fist thumping into bone. Charlie saw a tall white man fighting with Sam and Willard. They weren't on the bridge, but were in the mud rolling and pushing at each other. The man yelled out, "Run!"

And Charlie did. This time he held up the bottom of the cape and ran across the planks toward Georgetown. When he was out of breath, he dove behind some bushes, and waited.

Soon the man who had fought with Willard and Sam hurried past Charlie's hiding spot. Charlie decided to follow him and see who he was. If God had sent an angel to save him, Charlie wanted a good look.

CHAPTER

Susan's Tea Party

After his adventure on Willard's Bridge, Charlie was too tired to run fast. He followed the man who rescued him, but he stayed far behind him all the way to Georgetown. The gentleman walked fast, as if he were chasing someone. Charlie wondered if the man had been following him. *But why?* Charlie could think of no reason a gentleman would be interested in him.

Outside the general store, Charlie hid behind a large barrel of pickles. From his hiding place, he saw the man's face. It was a plain, ordinary face. Not thin nor too fat. Average-sized eyes and mouth. No missing front teeth. He didn't recognize the face, but if he saw it again, he would know it.

Charlie found the medicine shop and asked for the tonic and syrups Mrs. Briesler needed. After bargaining about the price, he paid for it and left on the main road. He ran the two miles until stopping just outside of town.

He avoided Willard's bridge. He decided to ford Rock Creek and come through the woods instead. He had no time to search for his pouch, for he wanted to get the medicine to Mrs. Briesler as soon as possible.

First he took off the cape. Then Charlie rolled up his breeches as high as they would go. He moved rocks and logs to create a makeshift bridge. He plunged across the Rock Creek, holding the cape above his head.

Walking back to the President's Palace, Charlie felt fine. He had gotten away from Willard and Sam, and he would soon prove that he could be trusted with money. Perhaps Mrs. Briesler would give him more work than just carting wood.

"It's about time you got back," the stout woman said when he appeared at the kitchen door. "Miss Adams is shaking the whole house with her cough."

Charlie handed Mrs. Briesler the medicine and the rest of the money. "Why is there so much change?" she asked. "You didn't steal the medicine did you?"

"No," he said. "It's just that I didn't tell them I was buying it for the president's family." He grinned, glad there was at least some advantage of looking and being poor. "My mother also taught me how to bargain."

"Aye, she did. You have a good mother," she said. "Have you found any news of your father?"

"No, ma'am," he said. "But I only looked in a few places. I'm sure to find him somewhere."

"Well, I'm glad to hear your spirits are up," she said. "Mrs. Adams has callers in the drawing room, and I've been busy serving tea. Can you tend to the fires on the top floor while I prepare the medicine for Miss Adams?"

"It's easy enough," Charlie said. He headed toward the

stack of wood he'd left earlier in the day. He picked up some logs and headed for the stairs.

"Charlie," Mrs. Briesler called. "Wash your feet first. There's a bucket of water just outside the door."

Charlie's feet would have been dirty from just walking to Georgetown and back. But they had an extra layer of mud on them from crossing Rock Creek. Seems he was always dragging in dirt. At that moment, he wanted his shoes back very much. A servant at the President's Palace should wear shoes. He shrugged. The only thing he could do was pray for shoes again, and since God hadn't heard him the first time, he doubted God would do anything at all. *The president's family is important to God, but I'm not*, he thought.

He met three workmen on the twisty staircase. There wasn't enough room for more than one person on the narrow stairs. Charlie had to back down to let each man pass.

He found Susan Adams' room by following the sound of her cough. As he started to enter, the door was pushed into him. Charlie dropped his logs, and a carpenter rushed past him. Charlie could see the man's back, but not his face.

The noise caused Susan Adams to look up from her play. She was sitting on the floor, but she didn't have much choice. There was hardly any furniture anywhere in the house. Her little tea set was there on the smooth wood floor; her dollhouse behind her. As Charlie stirred up the fire and added more wood, the little girl asked, "Would you like a cup of tea?"

Charlie looked and saw that there was indeed a large ivory china cup held out to him. It was not a toy.

The first lady's missing china! Charlie thought.

"May I see the pretty teacup?" he asked.

"Yes," said Susan. "But you have to give it back. It's mine, and so is the tablecloth."

"What tablecloth?" Charlie asked, trying to keep the excitement out of his voice.

"Here," she said and pointed at a piece of paper that was underneath the toy tea set. Charlie gently removed the tea set and picked up the paper. He could see it was a letter similar to the one he had been given by Mr. X and Mr. Z.

His chest tightened when he thought that an enemy had brought this letter. An enemy who had come close to the president's granddaughter.

"Where is Hannah?" he asked. Charlie couldn't imagine that Hannah would leave Miss Adams alone for long. Maybe a Frenchman had taken her or scared her away.

"Hannah went outside for—you know," Susan Adams said. "It's private. We're not supposed to talk about it."

Charlie relaxed a little knowing Hannah had just left to use the bathroom, which was called the necessary out office.

"Where did you get this?" Charlie asked, just as Hannah entered the room.

"Get what?" she asked, coughing.

Charlie held up the letter. "It's not in English," he said. "And it came with this cup!"

Hannah bribed Miss Adams with a lemon candy to tell what happened. The little girl told her story in bits and pieces in between coughing fits.

While Hannah had been outside, a tall workman had

come into the room and had given her the cup and the letter.

"He rammed into me with the door when I came into the room," Charlie added. "He made me drop the logs."

"Oh, fiddlesticks!" Hannah said. "I'm here all day washing and taking care of a child, hoping and praying for something different. I leave for five minutes, and all the excitement happens. Boys have all the fun."

She sighed again. "I'm going to take this cup and letter to Mrs. Adams right now. I don't care if she has visitors."

While she was gone, Charlie played tea with Miss Adams. He wondered if he had let one of the Frenchmen pass by him on the stairs. The workmen were everywhere. If a man was dirty enough, he could pass for a plasterer or carpenter. And suddenly he remembered the white laundry hanging from the windows of the Audience Room.

When Hannah returned to watch Miss Adams, Charlie said, "I think Mr. X and Mr. Z saw the laundry hanging from the window. Maybe the letter is demanding the money. President Adams will be so angry!"

"It's all my fault," she said. "Mr. X and Mr. Z are expecting to get their money now. When they don't, they may burn another building. And this time someone might get hurt." She brushed away a tear that ran down her smooth cheek.

"It's not your worry," he told Hannah. "God has been watching this country and the president, and He'll take care of it. I just wish I knew what that letter says."

"We won't be so lucky as to hear the president read this one aloud," she said. "How can we ever find out what it says?"

CHAPTER

Saved from the Ashes

Charlie and Hannah were still in Susan Adams' bedroom when Mrs. Briesler came in with Miss Adams' medicine. Charlie, Hannah and the dark-haired girl had been laughing while they were playing tea. "A merry heart doeth good like a medicine," Mrs. Briesler recalled a Bible verse.

Charlie stood up to leave, smiling at Hannah and little Miss Adams. "I'll just see to the fires," he said.

"Don't disturb the first lady and her guests," Mrs. Briesler ordered. Charlie wondered if she didn't want the visitors to see him because he didn't have shoes.

He left little Susan's tea party and added some logs to several fires. Then he went downstairs for more wood. Just then the president came home, and the Brieslers began to fix a meal for His Excellency. Charlie was hoping to stay around in case he could overhear the president and first lady discuss the letter, but Mr. Briesler wanted more logs to last the night and ordered Charlie to get some.

While all the mixing and stirring were going on in the kitchen, Charlie left to collect enough wood to keep the

President's Palace warm and dry for the night. He also wanted to look for his father.

The first place he looked was at a big hotel that was almost ready to open. Inside, Charlie found an old black man who was packing up his woodworking tools. Most of the blacks Charlie had met had been slaves, hired out by their masters to work at the federal city. But this man was a freeman like Charlie.

"Have you met my father?" Charlie asked the wood-worker. "A man named Curly Brooks. A big fellow."

"Curly?" the man repeated softly. "The Curly I remember would be about the right age for your father. And he was as big as a bear. But what I have to say does not make a happy story."

"You may as well tell me," Charlie answered. "I'll find out sooner or later. Bad news is no stranger to my family."

"It isn't as bad as it could be," said the man. "I've seen some freemen who got re-enslaved because they lost their papers . . ."

Charlie interrupted. "But what happened to *my* father?"

"Don't get worked up so," the man said. He laid a chisel down on top of a crate. Charlie noticed the man's hands had deep lines in them. The skin looked like mud that had dried and cracked by the sun's heat.

"He was working with the stonecutters in Virginia," the older man said. "His job was to move those big sand-stone blocks the builders used for the President's Palace."

"Is he still working there?"

"No," said the man. "One day your father must not

have been paying attention. And the next thing you know, a huge block fell on top of his leg. Crushed it right at the kneecap."

Charlie imagined his father's pain and sucked in a quick breath. "Can he walk?" he asked.

"Now I think he can, if you'd call it walking," the old woodworker said, rubbing his chin. "But I don't know where he went. That was about five months ago."

"Thank you, sir," said Charlie. He walked out of the hotel sad and lonely. His heart was also filled with disappointment in God. *Why did my father have to get hurt? God sends me help when I am working for the president's family, but when it comes to my own family, God doesn't lift a finger. God always forgets about me! No shoes. No father.*

Charlie still did his work even though he was sad. After making five trips with armloads of logs and stacking them inside, Charlie went upstairs in the president's house. He listened carefully at each door, but Charlie heard nothing about the second letter or the teacup. He went back to the kitchen where Mrs. Briesler gave him a supper of turnip soup and cornbread. It should have been warm and filling, but Charlie was still too unhappy from the bad news about his father to enjoy the good food. To him it tasted like swamp water and dried grass.

Mr. Briesler was there too, sitting down to smoke his pipe. He was full of news about Congress.

The first Congress in the Capitol building was to open the next day, he told Charlie and his wife. President Adams knew the representatives would have to travel all the way to Washington City in the snow. Many men would have to stay in Georgetown because few rooms were available in the federal city. And the rooms that were open cost a lot of money.

President Adams wanted to reward the congressmen with a reception, the old steward said. A reception that had to be put together in half a day.

"The good Lord help us," said Mrs. Briesler. "That's near 150 people, not to mention stragglers. How will we get it all ready with just the four of us, and Charlie without shoes?!"

In answer, Mr. Briesler simply patted his wife's hand to comfort her.

After digesting supper and the news about the reception, Charlie made one more round of the President's Palace to make sure the fires had enough wood to last until midnight. The last fire he checked was in the large oval-shaped room with the red furniture. As he scooped out gray ashes, he saw something in the corner of the fireplace. Hidden in the back was a piece of crumpled paper that had only been charred around the edges. The fire had died before the paper had burned. He grabbed the letter, and put it in the pocket of his breeches.

Then he left the President's Palace and walked the dark path to the stables, the old wool cape flapping in the wind as gentle snow began to fall.

The warm, pungent odor of horses hit him when he entered the stable. He had brought some matches and a small candle with him this time. He lit the candle so that he could find an out-of-the-way spot to sleep. Like the night before, the two footmen and the coach driver were asleep when Charlie got there. One of the horses nickered, but all else was silent.

He decided that he would be most comfortable inside a coach. As he went to the back of the stable, one of the footmen rolled over. Charlie's candlelight cast a glow on the footman's face. A regular face. No missing teeth. Not thin nor too fat. The face of the man who saved him from Willard and Sam. The face that had followed him all the way to Georgetown.

The eyes were open and looking straight at Charlie.

"So," the man said, "will you show me where Mr. X and Mr. Z are?"

"Why?" asked Charlie, frozen in fear.

"That's right," whispered the man. "I am Mr. Y."

CHAPTER

The Second Threat

A lump of fear the size of an apple caught in Charlie's throat. *I am trapped with Mr. Y!* he thought. He tried to cry out, but only managed to blow out the candle.

The footman, who was Mr. Y, grabbed Charlie's arm. "Shh," he said. "Didn't I help you on that bridge?"

The words and the man's tone of voice calmed Charlie down. Before he called for help, he would listen to find out why Mr. Y had been following him.

"Shouldn't we whisper?" Charlie asked quietly.

"Nay," Mr. Y said. "Those two fellows sleep soundly. In fact, neither of them woke up last night when you were muttering about fires."

"I was talking in my sleep?"

"Aye. You talked about seeing Mr. X and Mr. Z on red mounts. Did they hurt you?"

Charlie shook his head. "Why did you follow me?"

"I wanted to see if Mr. X or Mr. Z would talk to you again. You see, I've been sent from France to stop them."

"But you are their friend!" said Charlie.

"Let me explain," Mr. Y said. "At first the French government wanted them to cause trouble in the United States. But now the leaders have decided to sign the treaty that Mr. Adams wants," he said. "I was sent to stop Mr. X and Mr. Z. I took a job as the president's footman so I could easily keep an eye out for them."

"You didn't do a good job," Charlie said. "They burned down the War Department building."

"At least they claim they did it," Mr. Y said. "Now, have you heard from my two countrymen?"

Charlie decided to trust Mr. Y. He took the letter out of his pocket and gave it to the Frenchman. The man smoothed out the wrinkles. Charlie lit the candle again with a match. He looked over Mr. Y's shoulder and held the light for him to read by.

Mr. Y read:

"Dear Mr. President:

We saw the white laundry hanging from the window. We will come to you at the Congress meeting tomorrow and get the money. You will know us by the red flowers we will be wearing. If we don't get the money, we will ruin the congressional reception. There may be a fire started in your own house.

We are very near. We sent this letter with a piece of your china to let you know that we are watching you."

"It's signed 'Mr. X and Mr. Z.'"

The message soaked in. Charlie knew that the laundry hanging from the Audience Room was an accident, but Mr. X and Mr. Z didn't. "What will happen if the president doesn't pay the bribe?" Charlie asked.

"If there is no money coming, well, then a fire at the palace and then . . . war."

Charlie remembered Willard and Sam. Charlie knew how mad they were when they saw him again after he got away without paying. He knew Mr. X and Mr. Z would be even angrier with the president. He asked himself, *Would they really burn the President's Palace?*

"What are we to do?" Charlie asked.

"We?" Mr. Y said. "*You* will do nothing. I will find Mr. X and Mr. Z before tomorrow's meeting of Congress. There are not many inns near here. You say Mr. X and Mr. Z rode red horses. I will find the inn that has two red horses in the stables. Then I will notify the president. He is able to lock up Frenchmen without any reason whatsoever." Mr. Y folded the letter and put it inside his shirt. He packed a large cloth bag. Then he saddled a horse. He opened and closed the stable door carefully; he was so quiet that neither of the other men noticed.

Charlie crawled inside Mrs. Adams' coach to make a bed. A crate covered with a white sheet was on the floor. Charlie grabbed the sheet to borrow it for the night. As he lifted it up, he saw something peeking between the slats.

He pushed his hand inside the crate and pulled out something cool, smooth and round. A cream-colored plate. He held the candle right up next to it. The first lady's missing china. *Why is this here?* he asked himself.

Charlie sat up straight in the carriage and tried to stay alert in case the Frenchman came back, but his head soon fell gently to the side, and he was fast asleep.

This time he was too tired to dream.

CHAPTER

10

The New Capitol

Charlie woke up first the next morning. There was no sign of Mr. Y in the stables, and so he hurried to the President's Palace. As Mrs. Briesler prepared him a simple breakfast of oatcakes and milk, Charlie told her where she could find the missing china.

"To think we've looked in the stables at least four times," said Mrs. Briesler. "Well, no matter. We have the dishes on the day we need them the most. Today's the congressional reception."

After tending to the fires, Charlie went to find Hannah. He found her scrubbing floors in the oval room upstairs. From the doorway, he motioned for her to meet him outside.

Soon the two young servants met behind the necessary. The smell was worse than in the stables, but it was the only place they could not be seen from the President's Palace—and they certainly could not be heard.

Hannah came around to the back of the shack by

following Charlie's footprints in the snow. "We'll have to hurry," Hannah said. "I've got more work to do in four hours than I could do in ten days."

"I found Mr. Y," Charlie said simply. Then he told her what had happened in the stables.

Hannah stopped and stared at him as he told his story. Her mouth stretched open as wide as a yawning cat's while she listened in wonder. "You have all the fun," she said when he was finished. "I've been up all night listening to Miss Adams cough." Then she grew more serious. "I've got some news, too. A special messenger arrived this morning with a letter for the president. As I poured tea, the president told Mrs. Adams that two men were captured at an inn at Georgetown. They were thrown in jail because they were French. It sounds as if your Mr. X and Mr. Z are in jail. Maybe Mr. Y has stopped them. The country is safe!"

Suddenly Hannah smiled so warmly that Charlie thought the sun couldn't match her smile's brightness. "I've got to get back. I have to polish the silverware." And with that comment she was off and running to the President's Palace.

For some reason, Charlie didn't feel as safe as he would like. But he brushed the feeling aside. His part to prepare for the reception would be to find dry wood, which would not be easy since it had snowed three inches during the night. Not too far away, he stopped to pull branches off a dead maple tree. It stood near a church that was under construction. Two Scottish stonecutters were at their business finishing the walkway. Charlie asked them about his father. The men didn't remember the name Curly Brooks, but they did remember the black man who got his kneecap crushed.

"He'll be fine with crutches," said the head stone-mason. "We don't know where he could get work around here with a bad leg, though. Sorry, we can't help."

Charlie walked aimlessly after that. He watched his bare feet sink into the snowy paths that served as the road between the President's Palace and the Capitol building. He wished he knew what to do to find his father. *Where could my father work with a weak leg? Why doesn't God help me?* he asked himself.

At the Capitol, he stopped when he saw the gathering of carriages and horses waiting outside the massive building that was only half finished. He looked for two red horses, just in case, but none were there. A small group of military men huddled outside in the cold. The building's arched windows and columns gave it a dignified look. It was designed to be two chambers joined by a great hall. The Senate chambers had been nearly finished; the hall and House of Representative chambers were only at the beginning stages of construction.

Charlie wanted to sneak inside to look. All of the seats in the gallery were taken by businessmen, tradesmen, and a few women with large hats. Crowds of men stood in the back of the huge unfinished room.

Charlie had never seen so many well-dressed men in his life. Many congressmen wore white wigs, buckled shoes, and black coats. They looked grand. But there were also men dressed in deerskin. They didn't look as proper, but there was a wild toughness about them. Charlie saw one man spit his tobacco right on the floor.

The men in nice clothes didn't spit. They had little oval cases in their pockets for snuff. Every once in a while, a man would open the small box and pinch out some snuff. Some men sniffed the fine powder into their noses. Some would wad the snuff up and mold it on their gums. When they were through with it, they would put the used snuff in a special bucket called an urn.

Charlie managed to move through the crowd without letting anyone step on his toes, and he found a place against the back wall.

He had to stop moving when the meeting began. After some announcements from the vice president, President Adams began his speech. "I congratulate the people of the United States on the meeting of Congress here in Washington City, the government's new home . . ."

A break in the crowd gave Charlie a chance to move closer. He could barely hear with the wind whistling through the cracks in the windows. Charlie pushed through a sea of shoulders when he knocked over a snuff urn. The copper urn clanked to the floor, spilling a brown mess on a man's buckled shoes. Charlie felt a strong hand grab him by the shoulder. "Hold on there, young man," said a familiar voice in a hushed tone. "What are you doing here?"

C H A P T E R

Answers from Rock Creek

Charlie didn't want to get thrown out of the Capitol building for knocking over a bucket. "It was an accident," he said as he looked up. Charlie found himself staring into the face of his father.

Tears of joy were streaming down Mr. Brooks' cheeks. "I thought you were dead," his father whispered. He hugged Charlie with both arms until Charlie thought his ribs would break.

All at once, Charlie's father released him, President Adams finished his speech, and the men around Charlie took a short break. The crowds headed outside for some fresh air and room to move.

Charlie and his father stepped into a quiet corner of the gallery. Charlie asked, "Why did you think I was dead?" He studied his father. He was wearing a new servant's uniform with breeches, stockings, and a tight-fitting blue jacket that had buttons down the front.

"I was wading down by Rock Creek yesterday," Curly Brooks said. "I was fishing for dinner. And what do I pull up out of the water—a leather drawstring pouch. Inside were your mother's Sunday handkerchief and some coins. I knew it had to be yours."

Mr. Brooks slapped his son on the back and started to laugh. "I should never have trusted those two teens on the bridge," he said. "One of them wore your shoes. He said he found them at the creek and that you drowned while looking for your pouch."

"Why didn't you come home when your leg got hurt?" Charlie asked his father.

Curly Brooks gave his son a weary smile. "I didn't want to come home a failure," he said. "I couldn't farm with a bum leg. I had no money and no hope of finding a job in the federal city. Or so I thought."

"Were you just going to disappear?" Charlie asked.

"I may have, but God wouldn't let me," Mr. Brooks said. "I knew He would answer my prayers for work, even if it took a long time. Since God watches out for sparrows, He would look after me. So I lived off the land and slept in the woods until I finally got a job emptying the snuff urns here at the Capitol."

"You mean that God answered your prayers?" Charlie asked in amazement.

"Yes!" Mr. Brooks said. "I got a good job. When I thought you were dead and washed away by Rock Creek I prayed a lot. Seeing you here is the best answer I could ask for."

"I guess I got my answer, too," Charlie said. "It just took longer than I thought it would. At first when I could not find you, I thought that God didn't care about a poor boy like me. But He didn't forget. I've got you back; now all I need is my shoes on my feet."

Mr. Brooks laughed. "I can help God answer that one. I asked the toothless fellow how he knew so much about your death, and he got scared . . . he gave me back the shoes without a fight."

Then Charlie explained about his job of tending fires at the President's Palace. "We could use help this afternoon," Charlie said. "The housekeeper would dance a jig if she found out she'd get more help. And, the president will need a new footman soon." Charlie was sure Mr. Y would never go back to the stables. "I can ask the coachman if you can have the job."

Mr. Brooks slapped his son on the back again. "A job working for His Excellency! We'd make enough money to bring out your mother and sisters! That's another answer to prayer."

*   *   *   *   *

Charlie walked into the kitchen of the President's Palace with a load of wood. Mrs. Briesler had all sorts of cakes, crackers, and cheeses laid out in small pieces on fancy silver trays. She was hurrying from one pot on the wood stove to the next, stirring everything with a wooden spoon. Her face was sweating, and her white cap was tilted to one side. Charlie had never seen anyone work so fast and frantically.

"Don't just stand there," Mrs. Briesler said. "I need all the help I can get . . .". She glanced at Charlie's feet. The spoon she was holding clattered to the floor. "Are those shoes and stockings I see?" the housekeeper exclaimed.

"Yes, ma'am," Charlie said.

"Thank the good Father in heaven," she said. "And just when I thought He had forgotten help for this old servant."

"He never forgets," Charlie said. "I know that now."

"Before I forget, I need you to finish lighting the candles in the oval room." Mrs. Briesler was back to business. "There aren't enough lamps to brighten that huge hall."

Charlie obeyed quickly, practically running up the stairs in search of Hannah. He found her in Susan Adams' room. The two girls were dressed in their best clothes and playing tea on the floor. For once, Hannah's apron was clean and starched.

"What's wrong?" Charlie asked when he saw the housemaid's tired, sad face.

"I can't be at the reception," Hannah sighed. "I wanted to see all the fine gentlemen and ladies. But I have to stay with Miss Adams!" Her voice cracked as if she were going to cry. "The only good thing is that you can stay with us since you don't have shoes . . ." Hannah's voice trailed off as she looked at his feet. "But where did you find a pair? You look right fine all dressed."

Charlie explained about his father, and Hannah's frown turned upside down and into one of her splendid smiles. "Oh, but that's good news," she said.

"You'll get to meet him," Charlie said. "He's a federal servant now." As Charlie turned to leave them, he said, "I'll come to see you when I can get away. Maybe you can watch from the Audience Room. That way you'll see the gentlemen and ladies coming and going."

He could hear guests coming up the service stairs. He left the oval room, passed the unfinished grand stairway, and entered the family dining room. From the window, Charlie saw the president's carriage stop at the main entrance to the great house. Only one footman dressed in bright clothes got out to attend His Excellency and helped him cross the new wooden bridge that covered the muddy potholes.

Mr. Y had not returned. *He's probably on his way to France now that Mr. X and Mr. Z have been arrested,* thought Charlie.

Charlie watched the guests come by coach, carriage, and horseback. The few ladies who came wore fine long gowns with lace at the bosom. The well-dressed Northern men came with ruffles on their collars. There were also frontiersmen wearing deerskin jackets with fringe down the arms. Charlie saw one of them spit a wad of tobacco on the step just before entering the President's Palace.

He went down to the kitchen where he met his father talking to Mrs. Briesler. She nodded to Charlie in greeting. "This man is your father?"

Charlie nodded.

"You can be proud." She smiled, and then said. "I need the snuff urns kept empty upstairs or those men from out West will spit tobacco on my newly polished floors. That's your job, isn't it Mr. Brooks? The president sent you over from the Capitol building to help today."

"Yes, ma'am," he said. "I'm on my way up." His stiff knee kept him from walking up the stairs easily, but he climbed slowly and steadily until he was out of sight.

Charlie picked up a food tray and trudged up the stairs after him. But he was heading to Miss Adams' room first. He was going to cheer up Hannah. But when he got there, the room was empty. He made a quick search of the rooms in the family quarters and then remembered his suggestion that they go to the Audience Room.

As he headed in that direction, he found that the president's guests hadn't been content to stay in the reception. They wandered about as if they owned the mansion. Charlie heard one man say: "This party isn't up to the standards of Mrs. Washington. The Adamses have no sense of style or manners. I would expect better from the first lady. You know they lived in France for a while. . ."

Another responded, "Did you see how the food was just set out, and how shabby the servants' clothes are . . ."

Charlie felt a warm hand on his sleeve. He turned to find Hannah, her light blue eyes wide and bright with worry.

"She's gone!" she said. "I can't find Miss Adams anywhere!"

CHAPTER

12

The Secret of the Teacup

Charlie and Hannah stood outside the Audience Room staring at each other. Charlie was balancing a tray of desserts on his shoulder with one hand. "Miss Adams can't be lost," he said. "Where did you last see her?"

"In the Audience Room," Hannah answered softly, "I was looking out at all the guests. I didn't want to miss out. When I turned around, Miss Adams was gone! Do you think a Frenchman kidnapped her?"

Charlie shook his head. "Have you looked everywhere?" he asked.

"Yes, even under the beds and in the closets. Everywhere except—"

"Except where?"

"The oval room," said Hannah. "I'm going in."

Charlie followed her, still carrying the tray. The room was packed with congressmen. At the back of the room, the Marine Corps Band played lively tunes on their brass instruments.

Hannah found Miss Adams quickly. The girl's teacup

gave her away. It sat on a table near the window. A small form was behind the curtains, and tiny white boots could be seen peeking from underneath them.

The housemaid sighed with both relief and anger. "The first lady will have a fit if she sees Susan here. The girl is still ill," Hannah said. Then she stalked over to the window with Charlie following.

Charlie watched as Hannah moved the curtain back and grabbed Miss Adams' arm. But the child's free arm coiled around the curtains, and she would not let go. If Hannah tugged, the thick curtains would fall on them both.

"I won't go," Susan Adams wailed. "I want to give my cup to the nice man. I saw him come in while you were looking out the window."

Hannah didn't need but a second to figure out that the man who had delivered the second mysterious letter and the teacup was somewhere in the room. "Where is he, honey?" coaxed Hannah.

Miss Adams pointed across the reception hall. Both Charlie and Hannah followed the imaginary line her finger created. It led straight to a man bowing to President Adams. He wore a white wig with large curls at the sides and a black bow in the back. His fancy jacket had gold buttons and trim. There was a bright red flower in a buttonhole on his jacket.

Charlie's knees turned to butter when he recognized the familiar face. It was all he could manage to keep the tray balanced and sit down on a dark wood chair.

In seconds, Mr. Brooks had limped to his side. "What it is, Charles?" he asked. "Are you ill?"

Charlie hadn't told him about the mysterious Frenchmen because he thought all danger had passed. "I'm not ill, but I have been dull," he said. He looked at Hannah. "The china was in the stables the whole time. Of course Mr. Y had to be helping Mr. X and Mr. Z."

"That's right," Hannah said, "how else would they have gotten the cup? They had to have someone who knew the house and could watch the president's moves."

Charlie put his head in his hands. "He must have turned in his friends so he could get all the money for himself. He's over there talking to the president right now, and from the look of things, it isn't good tidings."

The president was indeed upset. He was a man known for his quick temper and sharp words. He called out, "You scoundrel! To come here and pose as my footman. And you dare to threaten me in my own home?"

Mr. Y answered him with words just as heated, but in French. It was difficult to hear them over the trumpets of the band. Charlie and Hannah had no idea what was going on, and no one had been watching Susan Adams. Suddenly she appeared next to the Frenchman and tugged on his jacket. When Mr. Y looked down, Susan held out a tiny teacup in her dainty little hands. "Please, sir," she said to Mr. Y. "Would you like a cup of tea?"

The argument stopped. The voice of the four-year-old had captured the attention of Mr. Y and the president.

"What is she doing here?" bellowed John Adams.

Hannah quickly grabbed the child around the waist and picked her up. Susan screamed, "Let me go!" and kicked at the housemaid. But Hannah held her tightly and carried her out.

With the attention gone from himself, Mr. Y looked around the room. So did Charlie. No men were coming to the president's side to help. Everyone thought it was only the child who had upset the president.

"Your granddaughter," Mr. Y said to the president in English, "is the only one who has treated me kindly. You should not have hung white laundry in the window if you were not going to pay us the money. Now the fires will not stop until they've burned every federal building and ship of the United States Navy. You have not seen the last of me!"

He turned and rushed toward the wide double doors leading into Cross Hall. The president's guests were too confused to do anything to stop him. They just whispered, "The French have such strange manners. . . ."

Mr. Brooks lunged at the running Frenchman, but his knee gave out, and he could only grab ahold of Mr. Y's jacket. The material slipped from his fingers, and Mr. Brooks landed on the floor.

Charlie had been quicker than his father. He raced the man to the doors. He was just about to kick Mr. Y's leg when something hard hit him in the face. Mr. Y had swung the door so that it banged into Charlie's side, pinning him for a split second against the wall.

"Someone stop that madman!" President Adams' voiced boomed. The music stopped. But it was too late. Everyone was too stunned to move as Mr. Y ran through Cross Hall and down the service stairs.

Five seconds later, a man's loud yell was heard

followed by several heavy bumps. Charlie thought it sounded just like oak logs slamming against the wall.

Suddenly Hannah came out of the stairwell; her cap was half on and her apron hung crooked. "He's at the bottom of the stairs," she told the crowd of guests who had rushed toward the sound of the yells. "I think he's hurt. Someone should see to him."

As several uniformed military men rushed down the stairs, Hannah walked back into the oval room where the rest of the guests were seeking information from the president and the first lady like ants in a sugar bowl. Everyone was trying to figure out why the man had run away and why the president was still so angry.

Charlie rushed to Hannah to make sure she was all right. But he didn't have to ask. Her pale blue eyes shown bright as two stars.

"What happened?" Mr. Brooks questioned when he joined them. "I don't understand any of this."

Charlie's father would hear the whole story about Mr. X, Mr. Y, and Mr. Z another time. That afternoon Hannah simply answered, "The gentleman should have watched where he was going. There's not room for two people on those stairs. I pressed myself against the wall so he could pass. But I guess he tripped over my foot, and down he fell. I'm sure the president's men will catch him now!"

Charlie looked at Hannah's small feet. He had a feeling that Mr. Y's fall was no accident.

Charlie laughed to himself. *God finally answered Hannah's prayer for some excitement,* he thought, *at just the right time to save the country!*

Did You Know?

While Hannah, Charlie, and his father are make-believe characters, many of the details in this book are true, including:

• On November 15, 1800, Mrs. Adams' coachman got lost for two hours in the woods outside of Baltimore, Maryland. A kind African-American passerby showed her coachman the way out of the woods and told him how to find the federal city.

• In 1800, people called the White House the President's Palace or Mansion because it was so grand. It was not painted white until several years later.

• Four-year-old Susan Adams lived with her grand-parents in the White House. She played with a toy tea set.

• The Adams' only two servants were named John and Esther Briesler. They slept in the basement.

• Mrs. Adams hung her laundry to dry in the Audience Room, now called the East Room.

• While John Adams was president, Messrs. X, Y, and Z did ask U.S. ambassadors in France for bribe money.

The men were not French, however. Two were Swiss, and one was an American banker. It is known as the XYZ Affair.

• During the first week of November 1800, a three-story building used by the War Department burned down.

• It took thirteen fires to keep the White House warm and dry. The Brieslers couldn't find any men to cut and cart wood.

• The White House was unfinished when John and Abigail Adams moved in. Only six rooms were completed. Workmen had the run of the house, tracking mud everywhere. The main staircase was incomplete.

• The first Congress in the partially finished Capitol building was held November 22, 1800. A full-time servant was needed to empty the snuff urns.

• John Adams was the vice president of the United States for eight years before becoming the second president. In 1776 he signed the Declaration of Independence and was a key player in the Revolutionary War. He had many other professional accomplishments as well. But this is all he wanted inscribed on his gravestone: "Here lies John Adams, who took upon himself the responsibility of the peace with France in the year of 1800."